Sammie's Back

Other books in the series

Starring Sammie

Starring Brody

Starring Alex

Starring Jolene

Brody's Back

Alex's Back

Jolene's Back

Sammie's Back

the girl who makes a wish
(but then really wishes she hadn't)

Helena Pielichaty

Illustrated by Melanie Williamson

OXFORD
UNIVERSITY PRESS

OXFORD
UNIVERSITY PRESS

Great Clarendon Street, Oxford OX2 6DP

Oxford University Press is a department of the University of Oxford.
It furthers the University's objective of excellence in research, scholarship,
and education by publishing worldwide in

Oxford New York

Auckland Cape Town Dar es Salaam Hong Kong Karachi
Kuala Lumpur Madrid Melbourne Mexico City Nairobi
New Delhi Shanghai Taipei Toronto

With offices in

Argentina Austria Brazil Chile Czech Republic France Greece
Guatemala Hungary Italy Japan Poland Portugal Singapore
South Korea Switzerland Thailand Turkey Ukraine Vietnam

Oxford is a registered trade mark of Oxford University Press
in the UK and in certain other countries

British Library Cataloguing in Publication Data

Data available

ISBN-13: 978-0-19-275377-9
ISBN-10: 0-19-275377-0

1 3 5 7 9 10 8 6 4 2

Typeset by Palimpsest Book Production Limited,
Polmont, Stirlingshire

Printed in Great Britain by Cox and Wyman Ltd., Reading, Berkshire

to
the one and only
Michael William Fitzgerald
with love
and with thanks to Hazel
for a great day out!

Chapter One

If somebody had told me how hard Year Six was going to be, I'd never have left Year Five and that's a fact, that is. Do you know what time it is? Twenty to seven in the morning. Do you know what I'm doing? Only sitting in the kitchen on my own, learning how to spell key words for a science test. A science test a week before Christmas! That's not right, is it? If I were still in Mr Idle's, I'd be tucked up in bed. Not in Mrs Platini's, though. She's not a teacher, she's a slave-driver, that's what she is.

'Isn't there anyone at home who can help?' Mrs Platini goes yesterday when I'd had to stay in at break to finish copying the words off the board. 'Gemma or Sasha, perhaps?'

Gemma or Sasha? She had to be kidding. My two older sisters were too busy hanging out at the bus terminus to bother with me. When they do come home I usually scarper before Mum launches into her 'what time do you call this?' routine.

Mum can't help with my homework, neither, in case you're wondering; evenings are for chilling out, she says, not doing the teachers' job for them. In the olden days Dad helped me with my spellings and reading but I don't actually see him until the weekends so that's no good for a Tuesday test. Before you say, 'Well, he could test you down the phone', he can't, because the phone's not working. The wires have gone funny because birds have chewed through them and the men can't mend them until January at the earliest.

I wish I hadn't thought of Dad. This will be our second Christmas without him at home and I don't like the idea of it one bit, especially if Mum and Gemma and Sasha are going to keep having a go at each other throughout the holidays. Dad was always the one who smoothed things over but now that he's gone it's just one massive argument after another. It's a good job I've got After School club to go to or I don't know what I'd do.

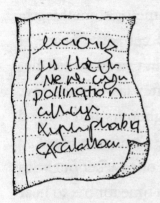

I glanced again at my word list, but now that After School club had come into my head as well as Dad, it was impossible to concentrate on spelling things like 'pollination' when this week at the club was going to be the best week ever.

I walked over to the pin-board where Mum had put the newsletter about the end of term activities, but just as I managed to find it between her Ross Clooney calendar and the ticket for her

Christmas Do at work, something prodded me in my back. I spun round to find our Gemma staring at me. Did she say, 'Good morning, Sam', or 'So sorry, did I scare you half to death?' No. 'What are you doing up already?' she goes, all grumpy.

'Homework,' I said, returning to my chair.

'At this time?' She sounded dead narked with me, as if I'd committed a crime or something.

'It's the only time I could get some peace,' I said, giving her a look. I didn't need to tell her why I needed some peace after last night's row. It had been that bad the neighbours had banged on the wall. Luckily, I had the Christmas Hits CD on full blast so I could drown one racket out with another. It had finished just in time for me to hear Mum giving Gemma a final-final warning that if she wasn't home by six all this week, she'd be grounded until next year. That had shut Gem up big time.

She was back to her usual moody self this morning, though. 'Has the postman been yet?' she grunted, going over to the worktop and shaking a box of Coco Pops to see how many were left.

'No.'

She made a sort of humph sound and grabbed a fistful of cereal and began munching.

'What are you doing up, anyway? Have you got homework to do as well?' I asked.

'Yeah, right,' she goes, her cheeks bulging like a gerbil's. Her answer didn't surprise me one bit. I'm telling you, I get more homework than our Gemma does and she's in Year Ten. That proves Mrs Platini's a slave-driver.

Gemma finished munching, rubbed her sticky hands on her dressing gown sleeves and then flicked on the kettle. While she was waiting for it to boil, she yanked open the bill drawer nearby and began rifling through the piles of brown and white envelopes.

'You're not meant to go in there,' I pointed out.

'So?' Gemma goes. I watched as she began flipping each envelope over, then scowling. 'She hasn't even opened half of these.'

'So?' I said back.

'So most of them are in red lettering.'

'So?' I said again.

'Sew a button on your head,' she goes and carried on rifling. 'Look at this stuff: Browne's, Elvyns, Clobber Hut, Littlemore's; she must have store cards with every shop in England. I bet she owes hundreds. That's without the utilities.'

'Utilities?'

'Gas, electric; the basics.'

'Oh,' I said, not one bit bothered. I'd rather talk about more interesting things.

'Do you think it'll snow this Christmas?' I asked her.

She shrugged. 'Who cares?'

Year Tens. What are they like?

Chapter Two

Guess what I got for my spelling check? Three out of ten. Chronic. That's before we even did the test. 'Did any of you even look at them?' Mrs Platini asked our table, peering over her specs at us when she gave back the sheets of paper. If I tell you I did best out of the four of us, you can tell why she might be a tiny bit disappointed. I smiled apologetically, Aimee carried on doodling, Dwight shrugged, and Naz said his dog had died.

'Again, Nazeem?' Mrs Platini asked.

'Yes, Miss,' Naz replied.

'That's the third one this month.'

'What can I say? We live on a main road. Poor Pooh-bum. May he rest in pieces.' Naz began wiping away a fake tear from the corner of one eye until Mrs Platini told him to stop being so silly, he was a Year Six, not a six year old, and we would all have to re-take the spell check at break tomorrow. 'She *so* fancies me,' Naz whispered loudly after she had left.

'How does she?' Dwight asked, taking a bite out of his test paper and mushing it up in his mouth ready for a spit-ball fight at break.

'She's always over here hoverin'—she spends more time with us than her 'usband.'

'I'm not staying in at break tomorrow—she can't make me,' Aimee muttered under her breath.

I just stared blankly at the three lonely ticks on my piece of paper and wished it was home time so I could get to After School club for some peace.

Chapter Three

It was a long wait, but the end of school arrived at last, and it was time for my two and a half hours of heaven. Some people think it's weird I like After School club so much. Aimee went once and said she'd rather watch paint dry she was that bored, but I love going. If my life's a sand- wich, right, then home is one slice of

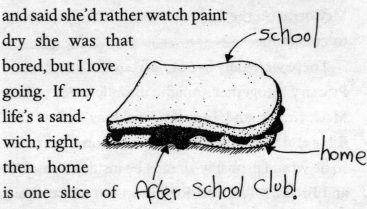

school

home

After school club!

bread and school is the other and After School club is the chocolate spread that makes it worth eating. In fact, this week was going to be so good, it was chocolate spread sandwiches with dough-nuts for afters.

Do you know what Mrs Fryston had got planned for this week? Check this out. Today and tomorrow is making gingerbread Christmas tree decorations, Thursday we join up with school for the disco—*groovy baby*—Friday we are having a Hunt the Christmas Crackers night. Next Monday and Tuesday will be quiet, wind-down days with a video, but by then it will be December the twenty-third! No wonder I was sitting with my bag packed and arms folded years before Mrs McCormack, the After School club helper, arrived to collect me.

There were only five of us from Zetland Avenue Primary altogether tonight: Brandon Petty, Alex McCormack, and Tasmim Aulakh as well as Sam Riley and me. Lloyd Fountain was home-schooled so he would probably already be inside the mobile and Brody Miller and Reggie would arrive about four o'clock when their buses dropped them off. They come later now they are in Year Seven and at secondary school. I used to wait for Brody outside the mobile but I kind of grew out of it. I'm glad I did because it was cold enough to freeze the buttons off a snowman today and her bus had to come from right the other end of town and wasn't always on time. It would be straight inside for me and no messing.

Chapter Four

Like a battery in a torch running down, the light was fading fast as we crossed the playground, but even from a distance the mobile hut looked cosy and inviting. The outside of the mobile's usually a bit shabby, if I'm being honest, but with fairy lights twinkling from every window and Mrs Fryston standing on top of the steps waiting to greet us, it looked magical.

'Quick, quick,' Mrs Fryston said, puffing out clouds of breath into the chilly air, 'get inside where it's warm. How are you all?'

Before I could say 'dandy', and that I liked her

earrings, which were long silver strands with miniature Christmas puddings dangling on the ends, Sam flung his arm across my chest, nearly sending me and everyone else flying. 'Like the kings in the Bible, we've travelled afar, to see *you*, Mrs Fryston, our very own star.'

He likes to talk in verses, does Sam. I ignore him; he can't help it.

'Very nice, Sam,' Mrs Fryston grinned as we all trooped past.

'Oh, Sammie, could you ask Mum to stay for a second tonight when she picks you up?' Mrs Fryston asked lightly.

'Sure,' I said, heading for the cloakroom as quickly as I could to get started.

Do you know, it took my breath away every time I walked into the mobile since it had been decorated for Christmas. It looked so brilliant. Streamers and tinsel mobiles hung from the ceiling; messages of Merry Christmas in different languages were draped across the walls; and we'd gone mad with the fake-snow spray on the inside of all the windows. Best of all, the settees and tables in one corner had all been pushed back to make way for this huge Christmas tree that was so tall the fairy on top was touching the ceiling with her wand, as if she was dusting.

I really liked the fairy. I called her Pen. Instead of being the usual blonde-haired white and pink thing, our fairy was black with a spangly, tight top and deep purple netting skirt, huge silver wings, and a wand with a red jewel at the end of it. She had long dark hair, too, that hung in lots of tiny plaits to her waist. Mrs Fryston got her from the 'Alternative Festivals' Shop on the Internet.

Brandon, who's the youngest kid who comes, immediately drew up a beanbag and plonked himself right under the tree. He'd sit there all night, mesmerized, if Mrs Fryston let him. I didn't blame him, either; I'd have been there myself if there hadn't been so much else to do.

First, I checked out how Sam was doing with the tuck shop, but he was fine so I headed straight for Mrs McCormack, joining up with Alex, Lloyd, and Tasmim on the craft table. Mrs McCormack smiled and passed me a mound of dough, a wooden board, and a rolling pin. 'Choose any cutter,' she told me.

I chose a star shape, a snowman, an angel, and a holly leaf. The angel cutter was the hardest to use because the wing bit wouldn't come out properly. I kept breaking a tip off until Mrs McCormack told me to dust the cutter with flour first, then it worked a treat. 'These will look great on our tree at home when it comes,' I said.

'Haven't you put one up yet? We did ours ages ago,' Alex said.

I carefully slid my holly leaf biscuit

on to the baking tray. 'We're still waiting for it to arrive from the catalogue.'

'Oh.'

'We're getting a white fibre-optic one for in the window. You just plug it in and it glows red and green and silver all the time. We're getting the extra tall so that's probably why it's taking so long to arrive.'

We were still waiting for loads of other stuff, too. Big presents for relatives and small presents for friends and teachers. Mum had even ordered a hamper full of luxury foods containing things I had never tasted before in my life, like ham in a rich honey glaze and handmade Belgian chocolates and plum pudding made with the finest brandy. I didn't mention those to Alex though. I'm not a bragger.

'A tree you plug in isn't the same as a real tree,' Alex sniffed.

Not as *good*, she meant. 'Well, Mum didn't want to be hoovering pine needles up all year,' I told her, not that it was nothing to do with her.

'We don't have a tree,' Lloyd said. 'We think it's wrong to cut them down for the sake of it.'

'What do you do then?' Alex goes to him, reaching across me to get the snowman cutter without asking. She's nearly as bad as Aimee Anston for pushiness sometimes.

'We find a fallen branch from the woods and decorate that instead. It's just as appropriate.'

'Where do you stick your fairy?' I asked, glancing over my shoulder at Pen.

'We don't have a fairy, we use natural things like pine cones and holly.'

'Oh,' I said, thinking I was glad I didn't live at his house.

'We don't have a tree, either,' Tasmim added, 'or a branch.'

'Is that because you're Muslim?' I asked and Tasmim nodded. I knew from Naz, who's a Muslim too, Christmas wasn't a big thing in his family. He said he was grateful for the holidays though and thought Santa was a 'fine dude'.

'Right then,' Mrs McCormack said, gathering up the greased baking trays full of biscuits, 'I'll put these in the oven and they'll be ready to decorate tomorrow.'

You see, that was another thing about coming here. There was always something to look forward to the next day.

Chapter Five

Mum picked me up at half five for once; it's usually way after six when she arrives. She beckoned me across and stood in the doorway as I fetched my coat.

'Hurry up,' she whispered, 'it's freezing out here.'

'Come in then,' I laughed.

'No . . . just get a move on, will you, babe.'

'Oh, Mrs Fryston wants a word,' I said, suddenly remembering.

'No time, no time,' Mum said hastily and disappeared before I'd even done up my zip.

I gave Mrs Fryston a quick wave, so she'd know I was going, and dashed out. 'How come you're early?' I asked, gasping as the cold air hit me as soon as we left the warm mobile. It was pitch black by now, and drizzling.

I held on to Mum's hand as she pulled the collar of her new leather jacket up and together we ran across the playground towards the car park.

'I clocked out early; I wanted to make sure those two remembered what I told them about being in by six,' she explained, fumbling for her car keys. 'Get in before you catch your death,' she said, leaning across the passenger seat and opening the door for me. 'Right, let's see where they are.'

'They'll be at home; it's too cold not to be,' I told her, though I didn't really have the foggiest if they would or not.

'They'd better be,' she said. 'It's time that pair remembered who gives the orders round here.'

Oh-oh, I thought, here we go. My whole day might as well never have happened. I left home this morning during an argument and I was going to walk straight back into one tonight. Dandy.

'Bridget says all Gemma needs is consistency; consistency and firm boundaries,' Mum stated, pulling away from the kerb with a squeal of tyres. 'And if I sort Gemma out, Sasha will follow. That's what Bridget reckons.'

Bridget? What does she know? Mum's friend was always criticizing us and Mum always listened to her, even though Bridget had never had kids. Still, it made sense, I suppose. 'I made ginger-bread tree decorations today,' I told her, trying to change the subject, 'I didn't get the icing done yet—they have to cool thoroughly . . .'

I knew I was wasting my breath. Mum was not listening to me at all, so we fell into this two-way conversation we often have on the way home, where we both talk about different things and arrive back believing we'd had a good chat.

Mum goes: '. . . Bridget saw this episode of *Ask Sally* last week when she was off with a migraine. "Have You Got A Teenager From Hell In Your House?" it was called. Have I? Not much! I wish I'd seen it. I told Bridget she should have recorded it for me.'

And I went: 'By the way, don't forget I'm going to be late home on Thursday. It's the school disco. Do you think Sasha will lend me her spangly top?'

Then Mum goes: 'Consistency is the key. That's been my problem. Lack of consistency; your dad used to say it, too, but I never listened.'

And I went: 'Cos it'll go really well with my party trou—' but then I stopped. 'What did you say, Mum?'

'What?'

'About Dad?'

'Nothing. I just said he was always telling me I was inconsistent. "Eileen, if you tell them you're going to do something, do it," he'd say. I know what he means now. Like that time . . .'

I was in too much shock to listen to her examples. Mum admitting Dad had been right about something? Blimey! That was a first. I began to get excited and my mind started racing. What if she thought he was right about a lot of things? Would she start to like him again? It can happen, I've seen it on *EastEnders*. Dad's not going out with that dozy Julie any more, so Dad was single,

Mum was single. Christmas was coming . . .

'If they're at that bus terminus, I'll swing for them, I will . . .' Mum replied as we turned into the estate.

Luckily, the bus terminus, when we crawled past, was empty. 'Mm,' Mum said.

Chapter Six

Trouble was, they weren't at home, either. They weren't that far behind us, only a few minutes, but it was enough for Mum to blow her top. 'Where have you been?' Mum demanded as soon as they walked in the door, but didn't give them a chance to explain. 'You're both grounded for a month, end of story.'

Sasha looked startled but Gemma, dumping her school bag on the pile of letters on the kitchen table, just shrugged.

'I mean it, Gemma!' Mum said, turning her wagging finger towards her.

Gemma gave Mum one of her special looks that would have withered me in a second. 'I haven't said anything, have I?' she hissed.

'No, and I wouldn't if I were you, neither.'

Let that be the end of it so I can have some spaghetti hoops on toast, I thought, but no, Gemma had to keep it going, didn't she? 'All right, keep your wig on. There's no need to take it out on us just because you've got the hump.'

Mum's whole body puffed out as if she was being inflated by a balloon pump. 'Hump? I'll give you hump!'

It was time for me to escape. I grabbed a handful of biscuits from the barrel behind me and pushed past the three of them. If the neighbours started banging again, I wanted to be well out of the way.

Upstairs, I lay on my bed and reached behind my bedstead and found my Walkman. It still had the 'Kids at Christmas' CD in it from last night. I turned the volume up to full and listened to some daft school choir singing 'All I want for Christmas is me two front teeth'.

Two front teeth? What a dumb thing to wish for. Having your dad back home: now that was a proper wish.

Chapter Seven

Guess what I got for my spelling check next day? Two out of ten. One worse than yesterday! Even Naz managed five this time. Afterwards, when everyone else had been dismissed, Mrs Platini gave me this mega long talk about how she knew it wasn't fair but some people just had to put in that extra bit of effort to keep up and if I really concentrated I could do better. She said I wasn't dyslexic or nothing, I just needed more one-to-one that unfortunately, because the class was so large this year, she couldn't give me. 'Is everything OK, Samantha? At home?' she asked finally.

What? Apart from all the rows and door banging and not having Dad around, did she mean? 'It's great,' I told her quickly.

She touched me lightly on the shoulder and said, 'Well, I'm always here if you need a chat, OK?'

I nodded. I suppose she wasn't so bad after all, for a slave-driver.

The rest of the day passed off as usual and then it was time for After School club. The first thing I wanted to do was finish my biscuits. I hate leaving things half-done, I do.

I had iced three of my biscuits perfectly, despite the wobbly nozzle on my icing bag, when Alex started talking about her dad. Apparently she was singing a solo of 'Silent Night' at her chapel's Carol Concert and her dad wanted to video her doing it. 'Mum, you are going to stop him, aren't you?' Alex began.

'Why?' Mrs McCormack asked.

'Why do you think?' Alex said, all mardy; she's dead rude to her mum sometimes, she is.

'I don't know, that's why I'm asking,' Mrs McCormack said.

'Duh! Because it'll put me off! And he'll show it to everybody who visits for the next seventeen years. Talk about embarrassing.'

'If your dad doesn't video it, mine will,' Lloyd told Alex, 'so you might as well let him; at least you'll be in focus!'

Tasmim giggled. 'My dad took pictures at my auntie Ambreen's wedding and chopped her head off in every picture.'

Alex ignored both Lloyd and Tasmim and began pounding her left-over gingerbread with her fist. 'Tell him not to, Mum, please,' she pouted. 'I'll foul up my long notes if he's whirring in and out.'

'He's just proud of you,' Mrs McCormack reasoned, 'and he knows how quickly you're growing up. He doesn't want to miss a minute.'

Alex snorted at that but she didn't know how lucky she was. I wondered how many minutes my dad had missed with me so far? Too many to count, that was for sure. The thought made me feel horrible and I knew I couldn't sit here, listening to people grumbling about their dads, for one second longer. I hurriedly finished off my last holly leaf and went to join Brandon sitting beneath the tree.

'You need to clear your things away, Sammie,' Mrs McCormack called after me but I pretended not to hear.

Chapter Eight

'What you doing, Brandon?' I asked him as I plonked a beanbag next to his and sat cross-legged beneath the tree's branches.

'Waiting,' he said, his face upturned and still.

'Waiting for what?'

'My wish to come true,' he whispered and put his fingers to his lips.

Something settled inside my tummy then, calming me down. I believed in wishes, too, especially this time of year. I shuffled up even closer to Brandon, until our beanbags overlapped, keeping as quiet as he was, and fixed my eyes on Pen the fairy.

I don't know how long I sat there, but the longer I did, the more I felt Pen could actually be magical. She was so pretty and wise-looking. I think I must have gone into a trance; you know, like when you're having your

hair braided and you're asleep but not asleep? I made a wish, too. It was the same thing I'd wished for last night: for Dad to come home. Well, you might as well aim high.

Do you know what? As soon as I made the wish, Pen moved. Only ever so slightly but she moved, she really did. I closed my eyes and made the wish again, only louder this time, but still in my head, obviously. Guess what? When I looked up, she moved again! She really, really did. I stared, open-mouthed, chanting the wish silently, 'Let Dad come home, let Dad come home', and then, before I knew what was happening, the whole tree juddered and Pen keeled over and flew straight into Brandon's lap, bringing a hail of silver lametta with her.

'Yes!' Brandon cried, leaping up and dancing on the spot with Pen in his hands. 'It's come true! It's come true! My wish has come true!'

Mrs Fryston was over like a shot. 'Brandon, have you been kicking that tree again?' she asked, shaking her head. Her earrings, pretend red and white candy canes tonight, shook with her.

'No,' he said, scowling and hiding Pen behind his back.

'Are you sure? Because it's such a dangerous thing to do; the whole lot could come tumbling down.'

'Wasn't kicking it,' he mumbled defiantly.

Mrs Fryston glanced at me but I was still in my trance and didn't say nothing. 'Let me have the fairy so I can put her back, Brandon, please,' Mrs Fryston asked gently, holding out her hand.

Brandon looked sheepish. 'Just let me have a look, first,' he said.

'At what?'

'I just want to see if she's got any knickers on,' he giggled. 'That's what my wish was—that she'd fall down so I could see.' *He* fell down then, laughing his head off.

'Brandon Petty!' Mrs Fryston said, laughing too. 'You little monkey! And I thought you were captivated by the magic of Christmas.'

'Well, my wish came true, so that's magic,' he protested. But Mrs Fryston was looking over my shoulder now and I'll never forget her next words as long as I live.

'Oh,' she said, 'your dad's here, Sammie.'

Chapter Nine

My heart was pounding like a pneumatic drill as I turned to see my dad standing in the doorway. 'I thought I'd just drop in,' he said, looking a bit bedraggled in his old wax coat and woolly hat. 'I hope I'm not interrupting anything.'

'Not at all,' Mrs Fryston told him. 'The more the merrier.'

'I had to see Mrs Platini,' he went on to explain, catching my eye, 'so I thought I'd come over and visit Sam for five minutes.'

Ah, I thought, so that's the excuse you're using. Good one, Dad. I mean, we couldn't let people know what really happened, could we? That I magicked him here?

'No problem, Mr Wesley,' Mrs Fryston told him. 'Will you be OK while I just return our escaping fairy to her post?'

'Of course.'

Mrs Fryston tugged at Pen's skirt hem and shook her head, still thinking about Brandon, no doubt. Me, I just went up and gave my dad the biggest hug in the world. 'Hi, Dad,' I sighed. 'I knew you'd come.'

'Did you?' he asked, sounding puzzled.

'Course.'

He shrugged. 'Oh. Only Mrs Platini told me she called me on the spur of the moment after school.'

'Yeah, Dad, right,' I said, winking at him.

'She told me she hadn't mentioned anything to you yet,' he continued.

I cupped my hand and leaned closer to him. 'It's OK, Mrs Fryston's gone. You can drop the act now,' I told him.

'What act?'

'All that stuff about Mrs Platini.'

Dad looked even more confused then but I put that down to being transported through time and space by a Christmas fairy. No wonder he looked bedraggled. He perked up, though, when I offered to show him round. We usually had to dash off together on the Fridays he comes to pick me up so we can catch the five-past bus. He never has time to browse.

I felt so proud, taking him round all the tables. Mrs McCormack told him I was the best icer she'd ever seen and Reggie noticed he was wearing his Wakefield Wildcats shirt under his coat and commented on that. 'Looking forward to next season?' Reggie goes and Dad went, 'Absolutely.'

By the time I had finished showing him round, Mum arrived. At first she frowned and asked him what he was doing here and he told her he'd been to see Mrs Platini and Mum went all pink and huffy and said, 'Well, she called me too but I can't just drop everything every time a teacher phones.' That was when I knew my wish had really come true because instead of Dad saying something like,

'Well, maybe you should', he just shrugged and asked for a lift back to our house. Back *home* were his actual words, if you must know.

'I think we need to talk, Eileen, don't you?' he said quietly. 'I mean, I can't phone to discuss things, can I?' Mum stared at him for a moment, opened her mouth, looked at me, closed it again, then shrugged.

'Come on, then,' she said, 'let's go.'

'Don't forget to bring your clothes for the disco tomorrow!' Mrs Fryston yelled after me.

'I won't!' I called, trying to stop myself from skipping out of After School club.

Chapter Ten

You should have seen the look on Gemma's and Sasha's faces when I told them Dad was home. 'What do you mean, "home"?' Gemma asked, throwing her bag on the kitchen table and frowning.

I put my fingers to my lips and pointed to the living room door that was shut tight. 'Home, here, back for good. They're just sorting out the details now,' I said in an excited whisper.

'Don't lie!' she goes.

'Go ask if you don't believe me!' I said, pulling back the metallic tab on a second tin of beans and pouring it into a saucepan. I was making tea for five. For five! Just as it should be.

Gemma glanced at the door, her frown deepening by the second. 'No way!' she said. 'No way!' She then marched straight into the living room, dragging me with her. 'Right, you two,' she said without so much as a 'pardon me' as she butted in to their conversation, 'just put Samantha-Panther here out of her misery, will you? She's got it into her thick head Dad's moving back in.'

'Well . . .' Mum began, scratching at a mark on the back of the armchair.

'Well what?' Gemma said, staring hard at Mum.

'Your dad is going to move back in, actually, this Sunday . . . just for a while . . . until we both get sorted out . . .'

'What!' Gemma exploded. Her face had turned as white as a wedding dress.

'It makes sense, Gem, money-wise,' Mum said quickly. 'You see, Dad's landlady wants to put his rent up in the New Year which means he'll have to give me less and I just can't manage on less, you know I can't,' she mumbled.

'It's not just the rent though, is it?' Dad snapped, giving Mum a thunderous look. 'That's the least of it.'

I guessed he meant the fairy and the magic and he was using that tone because Mum hadn't believed him. A deep pink colour was rising slowly from her neck upwards, like Ribena being poured into a wide glass jug.

'Mum? You are joking? Tell me you are joking?' Gemma fumed. 'You know you hate the sight of each other.'

'Gemma, don't be rude!' Dad told her.

'Well, it's true and you know it is. You can't mess us about like this, either of you!'

Can you believe my sister? Moan, moan, moan, whatever happens; good or bad.

Chapter Eleven

After School club was totally nutty that next after-
noon, which suited me fine because I felt totally
nutty myself. My dad was moving back home in
four days. Yey! Not that I'd told no one. I hadn't
had a chance. The club was tons busier than usual
for a start because a lot of parents had booked
kids in who didn't usually attend. I suppose they
didn't want to take them home then have to come
straight out again for the disco at six. There were
piles of clothes and bags everywhere with everyone
barging into each other and fussing non-stop. It
looked like a cross between our community centre

during a jumble sale and the backstage of a fashion show! It didn't matter, though, because it made it feel as if the party had started already.

Girls were queuing to get changed in the cubicles of the cloakrooms but the boys weren't bothered where they stripped off. In fact, Brandon was running round in his boxer shorts and vest chasing Tasmim with a piece of plastic mistletoe!

Mrs Fryston, wearing a Santa hat and huge snowball earrings, didn't even try to keep the noise down. In fact, she made it worse by playing 'Jingle Bells' at full blast. I loved it. I'm not sure Mrs McCormack did, though. She was busily trying to move all our gingerbread decorations out of the way before someone crashed into them. I don't know where Alex was.

I had managed to be one of the first to get changed and went to sit next to Brody on the dressing-up basket. She wasn't allowed to go to the disco now she'd left Zetland Avenue so she was just sat there, watching the commotion with a far-away smile on her face. 'Brody, do you think this top's all right?' I asked her. Sasha had been really mean and not let me into her bedroom this morning, only handing the thing to me two seconds before I had left for school, so I hadn't had a chance to try it on beforehand. It sparkled lots but it was a bit short and tight for me and I was worried that my tummy was sticking out too much.

Brody leaned her head to one side and took her time. 'Mmm,' she said, her tone so serious she began to worry me until she finally said: 'Sammie, you look totally cute.'

'Really?'

'Really! Girl, you are going to turn some heads tonight.'

I don't know about heads but my face turned as pink as a flamingo's feathers. 'Give over!' I told her, embarrassed but pleased at the same time. Brody's a model, remember, she knows what she's talking about.

She laughed and pretended to warm her hands

near my face. 'Ooh—nice fire burning!' she teased, then dived into her bag. 'Hey, you need some of this, party girl,' she announced, unscrewing the lid of a shiny star-shaped container.

'Oh, this is on my Christmas list!' I told her, dipping my finger into the jar of body glitter and spreading the sticky lotion along my arms and chest. 'What are you getting?'

'For Christmas? I don't know. Kiersten's so stressed out about the party on the twenty-third I don't think she's even thought about the twenty-fifth.'

'Oh,' I said, trying to imagine Brody's mum in a flap; she always seems so cool and calm when I see her. 'Why is she stressed?'

'Security mainly; she's worried the paparazzi will be snooping around trying to get shots of the guests when they arrive.'

'Why, who's coming?' I asked. All right, I admit I am a bit nosy when it comes to Brody Miller's lifestyle. Well, you would be, too, if you had a famous person in your group, so don't pretend you wouldn't.

'Promise you won't spread it round?' Brody asked.

I nodded vigorously and she leaned towards me and whispered. I nearly fell off the basket, I'm telling you. The names she mentioned! If you want to know who one of them was, just go into any record shop and look at the album charts or go into the children's section of a bookshop. Sorry, that's the only clue you're getting from me. I might be nosy but I'm not a blabbermouth.

Reggie, Lloyd, and Sam sauntered up to us then.

'Got enough gel on there, guys?' Brody asked, nudging me. All three of them were  totally smothered in the stuff.

'Should think so—these two pains have used my whole tube,' Reggie complained. 'Speaking of pain,' he continued, 'what *is* Sharkey wearing?'

We turned to see Mr Sharkey at the doorway, beckoning Mrs Fryston across. His white boiler suit did look a bit daft against the blue metallic wig, I must admit. The idea was he dressed up as 'Slim Shady Sharkey' for his job as DJ for the evening.

'How gay is that outfit?' Reggie asked.

Before we had time to tell him to shut up, Mr Sharkey put his referee's whistle to his lips and blew really hard. When he had some sort of quiet, he took hold of Mrs Fryston's hand as if to steal her away and grinned at us all. 'Anybody want to come with Missy Fry and me to the best disco on the planet?' he enquired.

Everyone let out this massive cheer and bundled towards them. I could feel the floorboards of the mobile creaking beneath us and glanced worriedly towards the tree, where the baubles were shaking. Pen, though, was fine. She stared calmly back at me with that secret smile on her face. Go and enjoy yourself, she said, and I did.

Chapter Twelve

I must have been tired out after the disco because I over-slept the next morning. It was quarter past eight when I woke up and I went into an instant panic because I hate being late.

Worse, when I went to get dressed, I discovered I had left my uniform in my carrier bag at After School club when I had got changed yesterday. My other sweatshirt was in the wash so I had to wear a normal jumper over my black trousers and hope nobody would notice. Talk about starting the day off on the wrong foot.

Downstairs, Mum was still in her dressing

gown, stirring sugar into her cup of coffee when I flew in. 'Did you oversleep too?' I asked. She was even later than me.

Mum gave me a confiding smile. 'Not exactly,' she said. 'Come and listen to this.'

I followed her into the hallway where she picked up the telephone receiver and held it to my ear. It made a buzzing sound. 'Oh, it's working again!'

'Yep.'

'How come? I thought the men couldn't come until January.'

'Well . . . your dad sorted it. Told them straight we needed it sooner than that. He was always much better at dealing with things like that than me. Anyway, to celebrate, I've made my first call already and phoned in sick.'

'Why, are you poorly?' I asked worriedly.

She smiled again. 'Nah! I need to do some Christmas shopping, seeing as hardly anything's arrived from the catalogue. Why don't you come with me?'

'What, and miss school?'

'Why not? I bet you're only colouring in and doing word searches. That's all they ever do the last few days. We can have lunch in the Ridings.'

I was really tempted, especially as I knew it was the science test proper today, but if I didn't go to school, I couldn't go to After School club. 'What about After School club? I don't want to miss that,' I said, opening a bag of crisps for breakfast and leaning against the worktop next to Mum.

Mum reached across and ruffled my hair. 'Suit yourself, sweetheart, but if I remember rightly you wanted that pendant for Mrs Fryston and all that other stuff for your friends and none of it has turned up, so if you don't get them today it'll be too late, won't it? How many days until the holidays? Two? And we can't do it tomorrow because I want to get ready for my works do and your dad's moving back on Sunday so . . .'

'You're right! I'll come!' I said instantly, the thought of not having presents to give to Brody and Sam and everyone making me more nervous than missing one day at school.

'Come where?' Gemma asked, sauntering into the kitchen.

'Shopping with Mum!' I said, tipping the last few crisps down my throat.

'What kind of shopping?' she asked suspiciously.

'The fun kind!' I said.

Gemma's eyes narrowed and I just knew she was going to say something mean, but before she could Mum bustled out to get dressed. Wise lady!

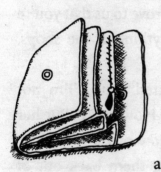

As soon as she'd gone, Gemma closed the door leading to the hallway and made straight for Mum's handbag. 'What are you doing?' I asked her, shocked, as she rummaged about until she found Mum's red leather purse.

'If she goes shopping it'll just undo everything,' she hissed. Quick as a flash, she fished out Mum's numerous credit and store cards and slid them into her pocket.

'You can't do that!' I said. I could feel my face

burning. We never went in Mum's handbag unless we were told. Besides, it reminded me of a bad thing I'd done once that I don't want to go into, so don't even ask.

'Listen, Sammie,' Gemma said, stepping really close to me and looking at me with wide, anxious eyes. 'You're always saying how Sasha and me leave you out of things because we think you're a baby . . .'

'So?'

'So now's your chance to prove to us that you're not. Don't let her spend anything at the shops. Anything.'

'No,' I said through gritted teeth, 'I'm not promising nothing like that! How can I? Put her cards back. Put them back now or I'll tell.'

'Right!' she said, grabbing them back out of her pocket and stuffing them where they belonged. 'Fine! But if she ends up in jail we'll all know whose fault it is, won't we?'

Talk about exaggerating. 'Oh, Gemma,' I told her, 'you're just jealous because I'm going shopping and you have to go to school.'

'Yeah,' Gemma snarled, 'that's exactly it, pea-brain.'

Charming.

Chapter Thirteen

We shopped until we dropped. Mum was in her element; her face shone as she chose one present after another. 'Isn't this brilliant?' she kept saying and 'Look at this! I've got to get this! I can just see Gemma's (or Sasha's or Bridget's) face when she opens this!' It made me laugh to see her so happy and excited.

Sometimes Mum's cards were refused so she just shrugged and offered a different one. The first time it happened, I was really embarrassed, but the shop assistants just smiled and said it happened a lot, this time of year. I just thought, well, if Mum's not bothered and the shop assistant isn't, why should I be? Mum's joy was contagious and I ended up as bad as her when I was choosing for my friends and teachers. Well, like she kept saying, if you can't go a bit crazy at Christmas, when can you? So hard lines, Gemma!

The one thing Mum did make me do was keep the receipts in a safe place. It always annoyed her if she found anything she had bought was torn or scratched or damaged; stuff like that went straight back and no messing.

I knew I had had enough when my feet were throbbing and I felt dizzy. I told Mum and she agreed it was time to call it a day. 'But not until we've had at least three muffins and a giant coffee each from Gingham's! Deal?'

'Deal!'

We managed to find a corner table and I sat and guarded all the bags while Mum fetched the coffees. I could see her grinning right across the food court as she came towards me. 'What?' I asked.

'I was just thinking how my mother would be

turning in her grave if she saw us buying all this stuff today.'

'Why?'

Mum carefully lowered the tray onto the small round table. 'Oh, she'd cut a penny in half would Joan; she was as tight as a duck's backside! I remember her making our Valerie and me go to school in wellies because she wouldn't buy us any new shoes. Honestly. She was always saving for a "rainy day" and what happened? Dead at fifty-three! Huh!'

'That was before I was born, wasn't it?'

'Yep, which just proves that life's too short and you've got to make the most of it. Am I right or am I right, babe?'

'You're right,' I agreed, sinking my teeth into my chocolate-chip muffin.

De-licious!

Do you know, that day in the Ridings was the best time I'd had with Mum for ages.

Back home, we had to scurry about hiding all the carrier bags full of stuff before Gemma and Sasha

came back. We kept
bumping into each
other and giggling.
'If they ask,
we didn't find
a thing,' Mum
whispered, heaving a midi hi-fi player into the top
of the airing cupboard. 'It'll give them more of a
surprise on Christmas Day.'

'OK. What about these? Shall I keep these in
my bedroom?' I asked, pointing to three over-
flowing carriers.

'No, you can't put them in there—your dad's
going in there. Shove them under my bed for now.'

'Dad's going in where?' I asked, just to check
I'd heard right.

'Your room. Why? Where else did you think
he'd be staying?' Mum said, wrapping a bath towel
round the hi-fi box to disguise it.

'Why can't Dad share your room, like he used
to?' I asked.

Mum scowled and grabbed the carrier bags
with such force I thought everything would plunge

straight out of the bottom. 'Ugh! I'm not having him near me! Your dad's coming back as a lodger and nothing more. And it's only until he finds somewhere cheaper to live and he's sorted out the bills. You'll have to share with Gemma and Sasha.'

'Oh,' I said. It wasn't the best news I'd ever had but I couldn't complain, could I?

Mum blew a strand of hair out of her flushed face. 'By the way, it's probably an idea not to mention today to Dad. We'll keep it our secret, eh?'

'If you want.'

'Good girl.'

Mum smiled and I smiled back. I'm good with secrets.

Chapter Fourteen

Guess what? Mum hadn't told Gemma and Sasha about me moving in to their room, either. Guess what else? They totally refused to let me move even a hair bobble into 'their space'. 'Put one smelly foot in that room and you're dead,' were their actual words as soon as Mum had left for her works do on the Saturday night.

'But you've got loads of room.'

'And it's staying that way.'

'You never used to mind sharing.'

'We do now. We mean it, Sam—stay out or else,' Gemma growled.

Charming.

'Fine,' I said, 'I'll sleep downstairs on the settee; I do hope neither of you trip over my shoes and break your necks.'

I just knew everything would be better once Dad moved in on the Sunday. He arrived late, grumbling about the cost of the taxi and grumbling even more when he saw the mess in the living room. Well, I'd run out of places to put things. It wasn't my fault if my soft toy collection had grown since he'd left.

'I don't know,' he said, moving Fizzy Cola the koala and Chyna the chimp so he could sit down, 'it's like the Disney shop in here.'

'Thanks, Dad,' I said, taking it as a compliment.

Mum wasn't there to welcome him home; she'd gone round to Bridget's to talk about the works do the night before. It had been a good night apparently. So good she had to go and re-live it with widget-face instead of greeting Dad.

'Probably as well,' he said darkly when I explained.

'This isn't going to work, Dad,' Gemma told him matter-of-factly.

'Tell me something I don't know,' he replied wearily, nodding as I handed him his cup of tea, made just how he liked it.

'Don't listen to her,' I said, offering him a biscuit. 'She doesn't know nothing about . . .' I was going to say 'magic' but I caught sight of Gemma's eyebrow, raised in a dare-you-to-say-one-more-thing way and I just said, 'She doesn't know nothing about nothing.'

Chapter Fifteen

Monday and Tuesday were the last two days of term. I was a bit sad because After School club would be closed for two weeks—it's the only holiday it shuts down the same as school and I'd miss it like mad, but the sad bit was totally outweighed by the happy bit. I mean, After School club is great but it can't compare to a Christmas magicked by fairies, can it?

All right, I admit we'd got off to a slow start at home and maybe things were a bit tense. For example, Mum and Dad hadn't spoken two words to each other yet. I wasn't worried though; I knew once the holiday proper began and Santa had been and that big, fat golden turkey was steaming away on the kitchen table and Mum and Dad had sipped a few glasses of wine each . . . I knew anything was possible. *Anything*.

I rolled up for school on Monday in a giddy mood. I had already decided I couldn't wait to give my presents out on the last day and had taken them in today instead. Mrs Platini was first. 'Here you are, Mrs Platini,' I said to her, handing her a gigantic box of Ferrero Rocher. 'Merry Christmas!'

'Why, how kind of you, Sammie,' she said graciously, 'are you better?'

'Better?'

'You were away on Friday. Were you poorly?' she asked.

'Yes,' I said, thinking fast, 'I had the runs.' Well, I did in a way, didn't I? I was running up and down those malls like nobody's business.

She pulled a sympathetic face. 'Oh dear,' she said. 'Well, I'll need a note and you missed your science test. If you'd like to take it home to do . . .'

'You'll be the first to know,' I assured her,

skipping off to give Nazeem his tin of Reindeer Pooh chocolate drops.

Soon enough it was the moment we had all been waiting for. Half three—After School club time.

'Did I miss much on Friday?' I asked Sam as we waited for Mrs McCormack to fetch Tasmim from Miss Coupland's class.

He pushed back his fringe and shook his head. 'Erm . . . no. We were supposed to do "Find the Christmas Cracker", but the mobile was such a mess from the night before we just ended up tidying.'

'Glad I didn't come then.'

'I found your uniform and things—I put them on a peg in the cloakroom.'

'Thanks, Sam,' I said, pulling him close to me and giving him a big squeeze, 'you are such a bangin' mate.'

'Eeek! Mind out, I'm delicate,' he protested.

'Delicate, shmelicat!' I laughed and squeezed him again.

'Someone's totally hyper,' he laughed.

'Course I am! It's Christmas! Speaking of which . . .'

I dipped into my bag and fished for his presents. They were a thick, spiral-bound notebook for him to write his poems down and a beautiful fountain pen to go with it. Talk about appropriate. 'Merry Christmas, mate!' I said gleefully.

'Oh,' he said, glancing quickly from them to me and colouring instantly. 'No, I couldn't.'

'What do you mean, "you couldn't"? Course you could.'

I thrust the presents into his hands but he looked really uncomfortable. 'I haven't got you anything, though. I don't do presents for school friends, just cards. I can't afford—'

'It doesn't matter,' I interrupted, dying to see the look on his face when he saw the things. 'Open them now. Go on.'

Still pink, Sam slowly unwrapped the presents. His eyes widened when he saw the notebook but that was nothing compared to when he saw the pen. He began blinking over and over again as if he'd got a piece of grit stuck behind each eyelid. At the same time, his mouth opened, then closed again, then opened but nothing came out.

Something was wrong but I wasn't sure what. *I* began to feel uncomfortable now. 'What's up?' I asked. 'Don't you like it? The man in the shop said it was a classic and it's got a five-year guarantee.'

Sam held the presents out to me like bombs about to explode in his hands. 'I can't take these, Sammie,' he said, his voice all wobbly.

I stared at him. 'What do you mean?'

'Well, for one thing my dad bought my mum the same pen for Valentine's Day last year and—'

'Yeah, well, don't go getting any ideas on that score!' I interrupted.

'It's not just that . . .' he mumbled. He was scarlet by now and I could feel my face burning, too, as Sam took a really deep breath. 'Look, Sammie, don't be offended but please could you take your presents back? I wouldn't feel right accepting them . . .'

His voice trailed off as I glared at him. 'Why not? Aren't they good enough for shop owner's kids?' I demanded, feeling hurt.

He shook his head. 'It's not that! It's not that at all; it's the opposite . . . they're . . . they're too nice . . . I'd only lose them . . .'

Too nice? How can a present be *too* nice? And as for losing them; Sam never loses things. He was just making up excuses and we both knew it. 'Fine,' I said, snatching them back, 'I'll give them to someone else.'

'Oh, yes, you must; that'd make me feel better,' he goes, his eyes lighting up instantly. Then he got his 'poem-incoming' look and went: '. . . Luxury gifts I do not seek; 'tis enough to see you every week . . .'

I rammed my fingers in my ears. If he didn't want my presents, I didn't want his.

Chapter Sixteen

I had a much better reaction from Mrs Fryston. She was delighted when I gave her my present the second we entered the mobile. 'Why, that's so sweet, Sammie,' she smiled, pretending to shake the tiny parcel. 'Let me guess? Is it a car?'

'No!'

'A jumper?'

'No!' I'd found her exactly the pendant I'd wanted; silver with a green amber stone. It was really special.

'Oh well,' she sighed, pretending to be sad, 'I'll just have to wait until Christmas morning to find out. I'll put it with my other gifts until tomorrow.'

I followed her across to the tree where she gently deposited my present with all her others. There was quite a pile. 'I know you'll like it,' I couldn't help telling her, 'I spent ages and ages on Friday choosing.'

'Ah! So that's where you were—Christmas shopping?'

I decided I could tell Mrs Fryston where I'd been; I knew she wouldn't mind. 'Yeah. Mum and me were at it all day. I thought my feet were going to drop off in the end! We nearly bought everything in the whole of the Ridings Centre!'

'Did you now?' Mrs Fryston said and although her smile was still on her face, her eyes turned cold. Only for a second, but I saw.

'Is everything all right, Mrs Fryston?' I asked her worriedly.

She straightened up and ruffled my hair. 'Of course it is. Off you go. I need to sort some things out. Erm . . . is your mum picking you up tonight?'

'No, Dad is,' I said, waiting for her to say, 'Oh, that's unusual', so I could say, 'Yes, that's because

69

he's home now', but she never. She just smiled tightly and said, 'OK.'

I never thought no more about it, to be honest. I wanted to finish giving presents out to everyone. They all took them gladly enough, too. It was just Sam who'd been mardy about it. Well, I wouldn't bother buying nothing for him next year, that was for sure.

Chapter Seventeen

Seeing Dad arrive like a normal dad at half past five made my heart do a triple somersault. 'Dad! Dad!' I said, jumping up and down and hugging him. All right, I was still hyper, but wouldn't you be? It was the first time my dad had picked me up to take me back home for nearly two years. You'd be showing off, too, unless you were made of stone. Or called Gemma.

'Wait there,' I said to him, 'I just need to get my stuff from the cloakroom.' He nodded and gave me a fond smile.

In the cloakroom, Mrs Fryston was helping

Brandon on with his coat. 'Oh,' she said, looking up as I began searching on the coat-pegs for my stuff, 'Is your dad here, Sammie?'

'Yes indeedy,' I said, squinting into one Londis carrier and seeing a blue metallic wig that was definitely not mine.

'I just need to have a word. Would you mind hanging on a bit?'

'No,' I said, 'I never mind hanging on here.'

'Thank you,' she said, patting Brandon on the arm after she'd finished doing up his last toggle.

I homed in on another Londis carrier. Full of someone's PE kit this time. 'Anyway, Sam said he'd put my carrier in here. He didn't tell me there were a thousand others, so take your time!' I told her.

She smiled at me and looked a bit sad, I thought. Probably because the club would be shutting for a while tomorrow and she'd miss us so much.

Eventually I found my uniform and went to collect Dad. He was nodding furiously at Mrs Fryston and his cheeks were flushed a deep, dark damson, but whatever they were saying to each other stopped as soon as I approached. 'Are you ready, Dad?' I asked.

'I am, love,' he said hastily.

'Bye, Mrs Fryston, see you tomorrow.'

She smiled, a bit awkwardly. 'Bye, Sammie; wrap up warm now.'

Isn't she nice?

My first walk home with Dad wasn't as relaxed as I'd imagined. He walked so briskly I had to run to keep up with him. I put it down to him being on nights; it can't be nice having to work when it's freezing cold and dark and everyone else is wrapped up warm in bed.

'Sam,' he asked as we reached the doorway.

'Yes?'

'Please tell me you didn't go shopping with your mum last Friday.'

'Erm . . .' Luckily Dad didn't wait for an answer. He just turned away from me and unlocked the door. I felt a bit wobbly then, as if I had really let him down.

As soon as we got in Dad began crashing about

with pots and pans in the kitchen. Sasha and Gemma were already home but Mum wasn't. 'She's at Bridget's,' Sasha told him when he asked.

'Again?'

'She'll get back when you go to work,' Gemma sniffed, 'you watch.'

Poor Gemma. She didn't know what I knew; that as soon as Pen's magic really started kicking in, Mum and Dad would be inseparable and she'd be making vomit noises when they kissed.

Dad scowled. 'Sammie, go into the front room and tidy up, will you?'

'In a minute. I want a biscuit first . . . I always . . .'

'Now,' Dad said brusquely, 'I want a word with Gemma and Sasha in private.'

'All right. I know when I'm not wanted,' I said and left.

I was tempted to listen in at the door but thought I'd better not. I didn't know why Dad was in such a moody all of a sudden, though. Unless Gemma and Sasha were in trouble at school again. Maybe he'd seen them mucking about with boys at the bus stop? Dads don't like that kind of thing—it sends them loopy.

'What do you mean, you don't know anything about it?' I heard Dad ask angrily. Oh-oh! My poor sisters. Dad was back now and on their case. They wouldn't be able to muck him about like they did Mum. I hurried into the living room and began tidying my 'bedroom'.

Chapter Eighteen

The first thing I came across was Sasha's sparkly top I hadn't put away. I thought I'd better hide it before she had a go at me. I sauntered upstairs and pushed open the door to my sisters' bedroom and immediately banged into something hard just inside the doorway. A quilt, but a quilt with something solid underneath it that made my toe throb.

I gazed around, realizing I hadn't been in here for ages. Wow! What a tip! Clothes and shoes and CDs were piled all over the place. And I was untidy?

There was no need for it, neither. Mum had bought them lovely new honey pine wardrobes during the summer and matching beds with under-mattress storage. Well, I'd show Dad one of us knew how to put things away properly. From downstairs, I heard the front door banging. Gemma storming off in a mardy, bet you.

I picked my way across to Sasha's wardrobe. The knobs had been fastened together with her school tie for some weird reason. It took me ages to unpick the knot. What was she doing? Practising for the Girl Guides or something?

You'll never guess what happened next. The second I had loosened the tie, there was this whooshing sound and before I could jump out of the way I was drowning in Jiffy bags and pack-ages. Dozens and dozens of them kept sliding out of the wardrobe, like pigeons dive-bombing for bread. One got me before I could duck out of the way—smack—right on the forehead!

I heard more crashing—this time from Gemma and Sasha as they burst in. 'Sammie,' Sasha began, putting her arm round my shoulders. 'Are you all right?'

Oh sure. Never been better.

Chapter Nineteen

I suppose you've sussed what all the parcels were? Yep. The stuff from the catalogue. Each parcel had 'Littlemore's—the family store where you pay less for more' in bold lettering across the front so my sisters couldn't fib when I asked what they were.

'But why?' I said, rubbing the bump on my head. It felt enormous—at least the size of a watermelon.

'Why? Why do you think? Someone has to stop her; she's out of control,' Gemma snapped.

'You're not on about Mum again are you?' I sighed.

'No, Bilbo Baggins. Of course Mum. Who else?'

'I don't get it,' I said, staring around me, 'how have you . . .'

'Managed to hide everything? Good question! We've been intercepting things for weeks. It's not been easy, either, dashing in straight from school before she gets back, collecting the fresh arrivals, and dashing out again to the post office. And not our post office, either—the one in town so Mrs Anscombe didn't get suspicious about all the returns and dob us in to Mum.'

I gazed at the mini mountain. 'Well, you haven't done a very good job of it if you've still got all this left!' I pointed out.

Gemma started waving her arms around like a demented wind turbine. 'What do you expect? It'd take Superman on Prozac to keep up with her. Look at this stuff; we've been returning things for weeks and you could still fill an orphanage. She's lost the plot!'

'No she hasn't!' I said. I mean, I knew what Mum had bought Gemma for Christmas and she wouldn't be complaining when she saw it, trust me.

Gemma shook her head as if she couldn't believe I'd said anything so barmy. '"No she hasn't" she says!'

'Well, she hasn't!' I repeated.

'Oh, hasn't she? Then how come you won't be going to After School club any more?'

My stomach lurched. 'What?'

'Tell her, Sasha.'

'Mrs Fryston told Dad tonight that Mum owes the club over a term's worth of fees.'

I didn't see the problem. 'Well, he'll sort it, like he did the telephone wires. He's better at that kind of thing—Mum admitted it.'

Gemma made a sort of choking sound and turned away so she wouldn't strangle me. Sasha had more patience. 'Dad's totally skint, Sammie. He's got nothing left after paying for everything.

He's supposed to go halves with the mortgage but he's having to pay it all which is why he had to give up the bedsit. He even borrowed money off Nana to pay the telephone bill. Bill, Sam; telephone *bill*.'

'No! Birds chewed through the wires—' I began to explain only for Gemma to jump in again.

'Oh, yeah, taken from the book *The Dog Ate My Homework and other Lame Excuses* by Howdumb Canuget!' she spat.

Seeing as Gemma was being such a cowbag, I concentrated on Sasha. I could tell from the look of seriousness in Sasha's eyes she wasn't trying to wind me up. 'Is it true? There were no birds? Mum just never paid the bill?'

Sasha nodded.

'But Nana's only on her pension,' I mumbled.

'Exactly, and that's just for starters.' She reeled off a list of other things Mum hadn't paid and should have. It turned out she was way behind with things that needed real money because there was nothing in the bank but she still kept getting new store cards and using them until they were maxed out. 'Mum won't listen—she thinks someone will wave a magic wand and make all the bills disappear,' Sasha concluded. 'Well, they won't, so we've been trying to make the parcels disappear instead.'

There was no need to bring magic wands into this, I thought, swallowing hard. 'And Dad's fed up with getting it in the neck for things Mum's done. Like the After School club fiasco. He's gone to work really upset.'

I felt horrible then, remembering the door banging. 'What did Mrs Fryston say?'

'She said they'd be able to work something out and they left it at that but he knows he can't. Look, he didn't want to spoil the holidays for you so don't tell him we've told you, will you? We're going to be in big enough trouble when they find out about this lot.'

'I wish I didn't know. I wish I didn't know about any of it,' I said miserably.

Chapter Twenty

As you can imagine, I wasn't the happiest girl around the next day, especially when it came to half-three, After School club time. Still, anyone watching me would never have thought I was all fizzed up inside. I joined in with everything as normal. I smiled at Mrs Fryston when she greeted us at the door and helped Mrs McCormack put all our decorated biscuits into green cellophane bags to take home. I even offered to help Sam on his stall, despite the fact I was still miffed at him for not taking my present yesterday. I thought I could cope if I did something normal like help him make a list of new stock he needed for the tuck shop, but Mrs Fryston clapped her hands and asked us all to sit under the tree. Oh-oh, I thought. The last thing I wanted was a group activity, even though there weren't many there tonight, Brody included.

When everyone gathered round, Mrs Fryston nodded towards Mrs McCormack who dimmed the main lights until only the fairy lights glowed. It made everything really cosy, if you were in the mood for cosiness. 'I thought it would be a nice idea if we had a kind of quiet circle time after all the excitement of the past few days,' Mrs Fryston explained in a hushed tone. 'I thought we could go round and take it in turns to finish my sentences . . .'

'Typical,' Alex whispered to me, 'taking credit for my mum's idea.'

'To make it more festive, we'll do it to music while passing round this parcel. When the music stops, you have to finish the sentence before you can unwrap the parcel. The first sentence is "The thing I'm looking forward to most this holiday is . . ."'

'Oh,' Alex whispered again. 'Mum never thought of that.'

Mrs Fryston nodded over to Reggie, who was in charge of the CD player. 'Music, Master Glazzard, please.'

Reggie pressed and Wizzard started belting out, 'Oh, I wish it could be Christmas every day . . .'

'Perhaps a little lower,' Mrs Fryston suggested.

As the parcel flew round the group, I grew more and more anxious. What would I say? 'The thing I'm looking forward to most is everybody arguing about money?'

Every time the music slowed and the parcel was near me, I almost flung it into Alex's lap. She didn't half give me some funny looks. Lloyd won the first round. 'The thing I'm looking forward to most is my grandma and grandad coming because Grandad always makes me laugh and shows me how to do tricks,' he said, a huge grin pinned across his face. Lucky you, I thought.

Lloyd then swapped with Reggie so he could join in and, surprise, surprise, he won the next round. Reggie checked his gelled hair was still as stiff as a clipped privet hedge then goes: 'The thing I'm looking forward to most this holiday is getting a new DVD so I can watch all my favourite films upstairs in peace instead of gay stuff downstairs like the Queen's Speech . . .'

And so it went on, with me getting more and more anxious as the parcel landed in my lap. 'I'm looking forward to going to see my cousins in Ireland in a naeroplane, especially if we crash into the sea and get eated by sharks,' Brandon told us.

When it was Sam's turn, he cleared his throat, so I expected a mammoth poem but instead he just said, 'I'm looking forward to Christmas dinner with my family.'

Finally, I couldn't escape. The music stopped and I tossed the parcel into Alex's lap but she tossed it back because she'd already done hers. 'I

. . . erm . . . I'm looking forward to Christmas dinner, too,' I said, copying Sam.

We went round a few more times with a few more sentences until finally Tasmim won the main present, a book of Greek Myths. 'Oh,' she said, really pleased, 'thank you.'

After that Mrs McCormack turned the lights back on and some of the parents began to arrive and that was it, my last time at After School club.

This is where you say a big 'aww' and feel sorry for me.

Chapter Twenty-One

By quarter to six there was only Alex and little old me left. I don't know where Dad was. Alex was helping her mum clean everything down on the craft table and Mrs Fryston was hovering by the tree. She turned and called Alex and me across. 'Girls, would it spoil it for you if I began to strip the tree? I'm going on holiday tomorrow and I'd like to get everything cleared up ready for next term. There's nothing sadder than coming back in January to Christmas decorations, is there?'

Alex said, 'Fine by me', and sauntered off. I

didn't say nothing. I was on full waterworks alert and had to be careful.

'Is anything wrong, Sammie?' Mrs Fryston asked.

'No,' I mumbled.

She looked from me to the bauble in her hand. 'I could just leave it. I don't want to spoil the magic for you; I know you like the tree.'

I glared at the floor. Mention of trees and magic in the same sentence wasn't exactly helpful in my no-crying mission. It was trees and magic that had started all this, I suddenly realized. 'My dad's late,' I said gruffly, to cover up my thoughts, 'it's not like him.'

'No, no it's not,' Mrs Fryston agreed, then sighed hard. 'Sammie, what is the matter? You look so out of sorts.'

'Do I?'

'You do and that's not like you; you're usually so cheerful. This is not the last memory I want of you before my holiday. What can I do to perk you up? Let me see.' Before I could say a word, she reached up on tiptoes and pulled Pen down from her branch. 'How about looking after our fairy for me? It seems a shame to pack her away during the most impor- tant time of her year, doesn't it? She needs a home to sparkle in! Have you got space on your tree for her?'

I hesitated at first. I mean, we didn't have a tree, for starters, did we? Unless you counted the one still in its box hidden behind Sasha's curtains. But Pen's tiny brown eyes held mine as if to say, 'Please take me home with you', so I said, 'Yes, sure.'

Mrs Fryston smiled with relief. 'I'll get some tissue paper and her box. You just bring her back after the holiday.'

'But I won't be here,' I blurted out. 'Though I could always give it to Sam to bring,' I added hastily, not wanting her to change her mind now. Having the fairy in the house might change every-

thing from pear-shaped to ship-shape. I mean—
my brain was racing ahead now—Pen had made
my first wish come true, who's to say she couldn't
make more wishes come true? Make all the bills
disappear, for example, including my After School
club fees.

Mrs Fryston was searching the shelves for Pen's
box. 'What do you mean, you won't be here?' she
asked.

'Oh nothing,' I said quickly, 'ignore me. I'm
just that excited about Christmas. I talk rubbish
sometimes. Oh, look, here's Dad.'

Chapter Twenty-Two

I put Pen on top of the box containing the Littlemore's tree as soon as I got home. 'What's that?' Gemma asked, looking up from her magazine.

'Just the fairy from After School club. Mrs Fryston asked me to look after it. Don't ask me why—I haven't a clue why she dumped it on me.'

I sent Pen an apology by mind-travel for insulting her. I had to play it cool in front of Gemma—I mean, she was the one who two years ago had told me Santa didn't exist and when he heard that, he didn't come again. Everyone knows once the elves hear that kind of thing coming up a chimney they move on. I still write to Santa, to show there's no hard feelings, but I couldn't risk her jinxing Pen as well. 'She doesn't even look like a real fairy, does she?' I sniffed.

Gemma had lost interest already. 'Yeah, well, it's better than being lumbered with the school gerbil, I suppose.'

'Yeah. At least fairies don't need mucking out. It's all right if I leave her here, isn't it? She won't be a bother.'

'Yeah. In fact, you can move in, too, if you want. You might as well, now you know about the catalogue stuff.'

'Really?'

'Why not? We should stick together, shouldn't we? You can help us decide what to do with it.'

'Honest?' I asked because that lumpy settee was beginning to kill my kidneys, I'm telling you.

'Yeah, just don't snore or you'll get a pillow on your head.'

I glanced over to Pen and gave her a thumbs-up. Now that's what I called a good start.

So the Christmas holidays began and that magic feeling continued. Not only were my sisters being nice to me, Mum and Dad were being nice to each other, too. It was all: 'Ask your dad if he would like a cup of tea', and: 'Eileen, would you mind if I took the girls to visit my mother on Christmas Eve or have you got something else planned?' kind of thing. That had to be down to Pen, didn't it? Who knew what stage they'd be at by Boxing Day. Chasing each other round the room with mistletoe like Brandon and Tasmim maybe?

That was when I let my guard down. Everything was going so smoothly, I thought I didn't need to make another wish; that After School club and everything else would take care of itself. I even forgot Pen was behind the curtain, if I'm honest, because I was so busy with other things. How daft can you get? If I'd made that second wish, I could have avoided everything that happened next.

Chapter Twenty-Three

I'm going to skip to Christmas Day now. I want to get it over and done with.

It began well enough, with Mum banging on our bedroom door at eight o'clock. 'Come on, you lazy lot! Have you forgotten what day it is?' she called, her voice full of excitement. I'm telling you, at Christmas, Mum's a bigger kid than any of us—she just loves it. 'Time to open those lovely, lovely presents . . .'

I didn't need telling twice! I was downstairs before you could say Reindeer Pooh Chocolate Drops.

Dad was already in the front room, holding a big cup of tea in his hands as I raced in. He looked a bit drawn. 'Are you OK, Dad?' I asked him. He nodded but still didn't say nothing so I thought he must just be tired. 'Oooh!' I said and I gave him a huge Christmas hug, not even minding his bristly chin. 'I couldn't do that last year, could I?' I laughed and he smiled then until Mum said tetchily, 'Never mind that—look at all the presents I've bought you.'

I turned round and nearly fainted. Do you remember Gemma saying the catalogue stuff could supply an orphanage? Well, the presents covering where the floor had once been could have been shared out between all the orphanages in England and there'd still have been enough for the orphanages in Wales and Scotland. There were masses and masses of presents; loads more than we'd bought together at the Ridings. They rose and rose like a shiny, badly built Egyptian pyramid. Behind me, I heard Gemma and Sasha gasp when they entered. 'Are these from everybody?' I asked Mum. 'You and Dad and Nana and Auntie Valerie . . .'

Mum shook her head. 'No, no, just me. I've gone all out this year to get you all nothing but the best.' She gave Dad a sidelong glance, as if to dare him to comment, but he just looked miserably down at his slippers. When I saw that, a feeling of gloom settled over me like a dark cloud at a summer barbecue.

'Now, come on, girls, who's going first?' Mum asked, bouncing up and down.

Without warning, she pulled an enormous box

wrapped in gold and silver stripy paper from the corner of the pile and held it towards me. 'Go on, Sammie, babe. You're the youngest; you start. Open this one; you'll love it!'

I don't know why, but my arm just wouldn't reach out to take the thing. Instead, I found myself staring at the parcel for what turned into a long, long time.

Anything more than a split second was too long as far as Mum was concerned. 'Come on, babe, open it,' Mum repeated. 'What are you waiting for?' She held the present closer, shaking it a little for good effect. I glanced awkwardly at her. 'Hello, anyone home?' she joked.

I still didn't take the parcel. I couldn't.

'Sammie, open your present, babe. Please,' Mum said, a hint of irritation in her voice. I just stared. The thing is, I could have coped with a few presents, or even our usual amount, but this was . . . this was scary. I realized how Sam must have felt when I gave him my presents: cornered and overwhelmed. No wonder he gave me the pen back. It had been totally over the top, just like this.

'Sammie? What's up with you?' Mum pressed again. 'Open it, babe.'

I stared at the present until the stripes blurred. 'I can't,' I said finally.

'Course you can. Don't mess about,' Mum said, a little sharply. 'Open it!'

She was getting angry with me now and I knew why. She needed me to react in the right way but I couldn't, just like Sam couldn't for me. She needed me to gush my thanks and tell her how brilliant the gift was. She wanted to see 'the look' on my face. How else could she justify it all? I glanced warily towards her. 'I can't,' I said again nervously. I felt shaky and cold; my hands were trembling. I was hurting both of us. 'I'm sorry but I can't.'

'Oh, suit yourself, Sammie,' Mum said finally and thrust my present back onto the pile and pulled out another one, similar in size, and gave it to Gemma. 'Come on, Gemma, ignore Miss Mardy there. Merry Christmas, babe.' Once again, Mum's eyes lit up with expectation only to be disappointed as Gemma shook her head.

More bluntly, Gemma put into words what I suppose I'd been thinking underneath. 'I'm with Sammie. I don't want my presents, either. I bet they're not even paid for—any of them. It's mad, all this.'

'Yeah,' Sasha added, glancing sadly at her pile.

Suddenly Mum turned and glared at Dad. That was when Christmas Day went from bad to worse.

Chapter Twenty-Four

'You! You've put them up to this, haven't you?' Mum accused him.

'Me? Leave me out of this,' Dad protested.

But Mum wasn't listening; she began to lay into him, her pointy finger aimed fully in his direction. 'You have! You've put them up to this! You and all your "let's be civilized for the girls' sake over Christmas." Hah! What have you been telling them behind my back? Kids don't refuse presents on Christmas Day; it's unnatural!'

Dad banged his cup down and stood up; his face was even paler than before. 'Oh, I agree with you; it *is* unnatural. It's also a sign of how much your spending's affecting them for them to go this far, don't you think?'

Mum shook her head fiercely. 'No, it isn't!' she said, but there was a catch in her voice. She turned to me again. 'Is it, Sammie? It's not down to me, this. You're just a bit tired, aren't you, babe? You'll open them later, won't you?'

'No, Mum,' I said solemnly, swallowing hard, 'Dad's right. You're frightening us.'

Mum looked as if I'd slapped her. Huge tears gathered in her eyes, building and building, ready to fall. 'Frightening you? How? I've only bought you things! My mum never bought me anything new when I was your age. It was all hand-me-downs and cheap rubbish from second-hand shops. Not cos she was broke, either, she was just too mean to part with her money.'

'I know, but . . .'

Tears were rolling freely down Mum's cheeks now. 'I always promised myself no kids of mine would go without at Christmas or any other time of year, no matter what, and you haven't, have you? You always have the best, don't you?'

Again, she kept her eyes fixed on me for an answer. I glanced towards Gemma for help and she nodded, prompting me to go on. 'But, Mum,' I said, sniffing back my own tears, 'we are going without the things that matter. I'd rather go to After School club than have too many presents.'

From the corner of my eye, I saw Dad exchange glances with Gemma as if to say, 'You told her!' Gemma just shrugged. 'Well, you can do both!' Mum flashed.

'I can't though, can I? You can't pay Mrs Fryston by store card and you owe her loads. Admit it.'

Mum's face crumpled but she shook her head again in defiance. 'Eileen,' Dad interrupted gently, 'you've got a problem, and until you admit it . . .'

Mum turned on him again instantly.

'I do not have a problem, apart from you, you big dipstick!'

'Mum,' Gemma said, 'come upstairs. I need to show you something.'

Chapter Twenty-Five

I had started the ball rolling. Now Gemma and Sasha finished it. Mum's eyes widened and widened in alarm as the parcels flooded out of the wardrobe and spilled all around her feet.

'I never ordered all that!' Mum protested.

'You did, Mum,' Gemma said, reaching under her computer table for further bags. 'And this,' she grunted, pulling at something heavy—the hamper, I think, 'and these.'

Mum's hand flew to her mouth. 'Oh God,' she said. 'Oh God!'

Dad was furious. 'Eileen! You told me you'd

stopped all this! When I agreed to give notice on my room and ask Mum to lend you the telephone money you said you were on top of things. You swore on the kids' life!'

'I know, I know!' Mum said, not looking at him, her voice almost a whisper. 'I know.'

'Look at it all!' Dad bleated. 'We're going to lose the house at this rate . . .'

Gemma rounded on him. 'Shut up, Dad, she's got the message! There's no need to go on about it.'

Dad opened his mouth but didn't say nothing. He just turned round and walked out. Mum didn't notice; she was just staring at the mess and nibbling the corner of her thumb, taking deep, anxious little bites out of it. Gemma went up to her and put her arms round her. Sasha followed suit, leaving no room for me. 'Oh God, Gemma,' Mum said, sobbing into Gemma's shoulder, 'what shall I do?'

It's funny, that, isn't it? Mum turning to Gemma after all the rows they'd had and Gemma hugging her back and sticking up for her like that. It was nice, though. It meant maybe Christmas Day wouldn't be such a disaster after all. Huh! As if!

Chapter Twenty-Six

Dad was in my bedroom, throwing his clothes into a black leather holdall. I thought maybe it was his dirty laundry or something. Mum had made it clear he had to do his own. 'Mad start or what?' I said, trying to shake a smile out of him. 'Shall we go have some breakfast? I can fry bacon now— and sausages—but don't ask me to do eggs because they make me puke.'

Dad turned to me. There was a look in his eyes I couldn't make out, but I knew I didn't like it. 'Sammie, love. I'm sorry. I can't.'

'I'll just make you another cup of tea then . . .'

His forehead went all white and scrunched up. 'What I'm trying to say is I'm going.'

'Going where?'

He gathered all his shaving stuff from my bedside cabinet and chucked it on top of his clothes any old how. 'Nana's. I can't hack it, Sammie; I just can't.'

'What do you mean?' My whole body shuddered, like a building before an earthquake hits it. I didn't like the sound of this. Not one bit.

He turned to me again and took a deep breath, then put both hands on my shoulders. 'I love you to bits and it's been grand seeing you every day . . .'

'Same here, Dad,' I said quickly.

'. . . but I can't live here again, Sammie. I should never have come back . . . it was a big mistake . . . big, big mistake!'

'No, it wasn't. It wasn't a mistake, it was a wish! Don't you remember? When the fairy magicked you into After School club that day . . .'

He looked blank so I dashed into Gemma's room, grabbed Pen, and dashed back again. 'Here she is! Pen, the fairy. She made us a family again!'

Dad still looked blank so I tried to explain but I was rushing the words too much and I knew it sounded far-fetched and silly and I'm a Year Six and shouldn't even believe in fairies but . . . 'Don't laugh,' I said, 'because it's true.'

He didn't laugh. He frowned at Pen a bit but he didn't laugh. 'Well, when I came to see Mrs Platini that day it wasn't really magic, love, it was a coincidence.'

'No!' I shouted. 'It was magic and you know it!'

'Fine! Fine!' Dad said hurriedly, throwing his hands up. 'It was magic. I see where you're coming from, Sammie. You made a wish and it came true. I did come home. You're right! Spot-on, in fact.'

I sighed with relief, but I shouldn't have because his next words weren't anything to feel relieved about.

'But now I've got to go again. I know it seems harsh on Christmas Day but seeing all that stuff . . . Jesus! If I stay I'll lose it completely with her.'

'But she's really sorry now, you know she is. You saw her face . . .'

Dad began to zip up his holdall. 'I know, I know, but it's not just the money issue . . .'

'What then? You just said it was nice to be home.'

'With you and Gemma and Sasha, yes, but being with your mother is like . . . is like . . .' He searched the room frantically until his eyes rested on my class photo. 'Is like you having to be with Aimee Anston every day; not only in school but at home too . . . and on top of that you have to give her all your things knowing she won't look after them.'

That stunned me. He knows I can't stand Aimee Anston. 'That bad?' I said.

He nodded. 'And to be fair it's the same for Eileen, only the other way round. All the magic in the world couldn't bring your mum and me back together again, Sammie. I'm sorry, but it can't. There's nothing there for the fairies to work on. Not even pretty ones like yours.' Dad leaned across and gave Pen a little tug on one of her plaits.

I felt sick, as if I'd been punched hard in the stomach. 'But if you go to Nana's, I won't see you properly. She lives two buses away and never goes out and always interrupts everyone's conversations.'

Dad gave me a weak smile because he knew it was a fact. 'Well, if your mum gets her act together I'll be able to use my wages on a nice big room somewhere.'

'That'll take months! Years! What about until then?'

'We'll work something out.'

'Promise?'

'Promise.'

So that's when I knew I had to let him go, because I didn't want my dad to be unhappy.

Chapter Twenty-Seven

What do you mean, how did I feel? Give me a break! How would you feel if your dad walked out on you on Christmas Day? Exactly, so why ask? I don't want to talk about it. I'll talk about Mum instead because she's the one who changed the most.

The shock of what had happened on Christmas Day turned her into this madwoman on a mission. Dressed in this revolting old purple and white shell-suit, 'to show I mean business', she made us come with her, day after day, to return all the stuff to the shops. Yep—all of it—every last little thing.

For the rest of the holiday we traipsed round one shopping centre after another, handing over things in crumpled carriers, turning away while the cashier examined what was inside before crediting Mum's card. After that, we started on the Littlemore's stuff, filling in return form after return form and making one trip after another to Mrs Anscombe in the post office who looked at us as if we were winding her up with all the extra work.

Finally, Mum made Gemma create a database on the computer of everything in the bill drawer and work out a list of priorities. Paying back Nana was number one and my After School club fees were number fifteen. Being number fifteen made my heart sink a bit.

Gemma and Sasha were worried Mum would crack after a couple of days, like she does when she starts a diet. You know, she starts off being good and only eating salads but by the end of the first week she's having just a few biscuits . . . They thought she'd be the same with the money, but by the time the holidays ended she had found an extra job in the Rose and Crown three nights a week and told Bridget she wouldn't be going out with her no more. Bridget didn't take the news too well and Mum told her there was nothing to stop her coming round to watch a video, but Bridget said the domestic thing wasn't her idea of a fun night out so Mum said, 'Suit yourself—good luck in finding another mug to sponge off.' I wish I'd seen Widget's face when she told her, I really do.

The night before we started school, Mum called us all into the kitchen. 'I want you all to witness this,' she said solemnly, 'my New Year's Resolution.' Do you know what she did? She cut up all her store cards and credit cards, one by one, right in front of us. 'There,' she goes, pulling a face like a kid drinking nasty medicine each time she snipped.

'Go, Mum!' Gemma yelled at the top of her voice as we all gave her a round of applause.

So that was it: the end of the holiday. Mum was sorted. Dad was sorted. Gemma and Sasha were sorted. And I was . . . I don't know what I was.

Chapter Twenty-Eight

I walked very, very slowly to school the next day. Snails could have overtaken me easy but I was too busy thinking 'what if' questions to have noticed. Questions like: What if people asked what I'd got for Christmas? What would I say? What if Aimee knew about Dad leaving again? She had a way of finding out everything that went on round our estate. Well, one snide comment from her and I'd punch her lights out and no messing.

Luckily, she wasn't there. Flu bug or something. Naz helped, too. He said he didn't want one word about Christmas. 'No rubbing it in about what you all got, guys, OK? It's not cool.'

'Fine by me,' I agreed.

I had been a bit wobbly about what would happen when Mrs McCormack came to collect the After School club kids and I couldn't go. Would they all stare? When it came to it, though, and Sam didn't even glance towards me, I wasn't that bothered to be honest. I'd had all day to think about it, see.

No, as Sam disappeared out of the classroom without me all I felt was a bucketful of relief. Can you imagine if Mrs Fryston had another circle time planned for today? 'Tell us all about your holiday, everybody.' There'd be Sam describing his fabulous Christmas dinner surrounded by his family. In rhyme, probably. 'Turkey breast filled with zest . . .'

Then there'd be Brody talking about her party, which, I supposed, had been brilliant. Next, Alex would recall her dad videoing her singing and I'd be so upset because that would remind me what my dad was doing at the same time. Not to mention Lloyd going all soppy about the tricks his grandad showed him. Mrs Fryston would smile and laugh at their happy little stories and then she'd turn to me and say: 'And what about you, Sammie?' But then she'd have a shock because Sammie would already have legged it over the playing fields.

No, I was really, really glad I didn't have to go to that poky old mobile hut for two hours a night, ever again.

Chapter Twenty-Nine

From then on, I had a new routine. At school, I avoided anything to do with After School club. I blanked Sam, Alex, Brandon, Tasmim, and anyone else who attended whenever I met them in corridors or classrooms. When Mrs Fryston came in to assembly to announce forthcoming events, I looked at the parquet and sang a song in my head. I always kept half an ear out for if she asked to see me afterwards, though—you know—wondering where Pen was. I haven't mentioned Pen much since Christmas Day, have I? I'm not telling you why, either. That's for me to know and you to find out. Anyway, Mrs Fryston never did ask. I supposed because I was just an 'ex' now; someone who once came to her club but didn't no more so that was that.

At home time, when Mrs McCormack called to collect those who had been booked in, I stuck my head in a book or tidied my tray. I had the tidiest tray in class by the end of the first week.

Avoiding takes up a lot of energy, though. I didn't have much left for concentrating on work-sheets and stuff in class. Course, Mrs Platini was down on me like a ton of bricks. I felt like telling her to pick on somebody her own size. Somebody like Sam Riley who could take it because he had nothing else to worry about except his dumb poems and his dumb tuck shop.

The new routine at home was this: I came in, watched telly, helped Gemma and Sasha make dinner. Dad phoned. I talked to him for about five minutes. Mum came home, had her dinner, then went out again to work at the pub. Exciting stuff or what?

Do you remember I once said my life was like a sandwich with home one slice of bread and school the other slice and After School club the chocolate spread in the middle? Do you know what my life was now? That last crust in the bread bin that's gone mouldy, that's what.

Chapter Thirty

In early February, we had a parents' evening. I don't know what parents' evenings are like at your school but at ours each teacher sits in their classroom and talks to the parents in turn. To stop you getting bored while you wait outside, they leave your tray on a table in the hallway for your parents to look through and when they've done that there are displays of artwork and field trips. Mr Sharkey hangs around in case anyone has a complaint or a query and sometimes parents put on refreshments.

Dad was taking me to mine because Mum was

working. I wasn't that keen on going because I knew Mrs Platini was going to give me a cruddy report, but it was the first chance I'd had to be with Dad mid-week for ages, so I went. 'I think I should tell you to expect the worst, Dad,' I whispered as we entered the hall.

He smiled, thinking I was kidding. 'Thanks for the warning,' he said.

I wish I'd had a warning. Then I wouldn't have nearly fainted when I saw the After School club stall. There it was, smack bang between the wall bars and my classroom, catching the eye as soon as you walked in the door. There were Mrs Fryston and Mrs McCormack, beaming away, wearing their ZAPS After School Club sweatshirts, giving out brochures and newsletters as people passed. Worse still, Brody, Sam, and Alex were helping them. My stomach plunged a hundred metres. I hadn't seen Brody properly since we were getting ready for the school disco. Our eyes locked and she let out this squeal and came running across to me.

'Sammie! Sammie! Sammie! I've missed you so

much! When are you coming back?' She threw her arms round me and started hugging me. For a skinny twelve year old, she's got a powerful grip.

I didn't know what to do. I just stood there and let her squeeze the life out of me.

Dad looked at us thoughtfully. 'Why don't you catch up with your friends? It might be an idea if I see Mrs Platini on my own anyway,' he said.

Brody squeezed again. 'Neat! Come on.'

She dragged me towards the After School club table. 'Look who I found!' she announced.

'Sammie! It's lovely to see you,' Mrs Fryston said. 'Did you have a good Christmas?'

Of all the flipping questions in all the flipping world she would have to open with that one, wouldn't she? Do you know what I did? I burst into tears! I don't know where they came from or why they had to choose that moment, but I was sobbing my heart out in seconds. Talk about embarrassing.

The trouble with me, you see, is once I start I can't stop. The last time I'd cried like this was in summer, when I'd had a fight with Jolene Nevin.

I'd used up two boxes of tissues within about a minute. I wouldn't mind, but that was after I'd won!

Mrs Fryston must have thought I was nuts, but she rushed round the display table immediately and gave me a hug. 'Oh no, don't cry! Look,' she said, fishing inside the collar of her sweatshirt and showing me the pendant I bought her to distract me, 'I wear it all the time. Thank you so much!'

That just made it worse! I cried harder then, thinking if Mum saw that it'd be snatched off her neck and back in H. Samuel's before you could blink.

'S . . . sorry,' I wept, glancing up first at Mrs Fryston then at everyone else's stunned faces.

'Was it that bad?' Brody asked, but I could only manage a nod.

'If it helps, mine wasn't great,' Brody goes. 'You remember I told you we were having a party? Well, my dad found a reporter hiding in the shrubbery, snapping away as the guests arrived. Jake totally freaked and chinned the guy as well as smashing his camera, so the guy's suing *us* for damages. It is *so* not the kind of publicity we need.'

I managed a feeble 'oh', and blew into a tissue.

'And we got flooded out,' Sam said miserably.

I looked at Sam properly for the first time in weeks. I'd been kind of avoiding him, as you know. I was surprised to see how fed up he seemed. His shoulders drooped and his voice was flat, as if even talking was an effort. 'W-what do you m-mean?' I mumbled.

He sighed hard. 'A burst water-main in the arcade flooded our shop and two others. Everything was ruined.'

'Oh no!' I wailed, knowing how proud Sam was of the card shop his parents ran.

Mrs Fryston bustled me round the back of the stall to join him. 'He spent Christmas Day up to his knees in water surrounded by soggy calendars, didn't you, you poor thing?'

'D . . . didn't you get your Christmas dinner then?' I sniffed.

'If you call cheese on toast Christmas dinner, then yes.'

'I'm sorry,' I said again, feeling bad for being jealous of him before and even worse for the spiteful things I'd wished on him. How could I have been so mean? This was Sam, who had been my best friend at After School club for over a year. What was I thinking? 'All I had were the gingerbread decorations,' I confessed.

Sam gave a bleak smile and I half expected Alex to butt in and tell me we weren't meant to eat them, but she just raised one eyebrow a tiny bit higher, that's all. 'Lloyd's was the worst Christmas though, I think,' she said.

'Why? What happened to Lloyd?' I asked.

Her voice wobbled. 'His grandad died,' she said quietly.

My sobs stopped then. Instantly.

Alex was about to explain what had happened when Dad arrived, and he didn't look very happy.

'I'd better go,' I said, edging my way from the

back of the stall and wiping my face with the back of my hand.

'Oh, take a brochure and a newsletter with you, Sammie,' Mrs Fryston said, pressing them upon me. 'There's a lovely picture of you playing football last summer.' She smiled at Dad who just nodded briefly.

'Thanks,' I said, 'thanks—bye.'

I hurried after Dad, not looking back. I'd only have wanted to stay.

Chapter Thirty-One

Outside, I slid my arm through Dad's and tried to match his walk, stride for stride. 'Hey, Dad, you know we thought we had a grotty Christmas? Well, we weren't the only ones! Lloyd Fountain, right—'

'Forget Christmas!' Dad snapped. 'It's now that's important. Mrs Platini's just given me a right ear-bashing about you! What are you playing at?'

I groaned. I didn't want to talk about her. I wanted to talk about Lloyd.

'She says you're not paying attention in class, you're uncooperative, you don't finish work when she'd asked you . . . and that's just for starters! I'm really, really disappointed in you.'

'I told you not to expect anything good,' I said sulkily.

'Sammie!' Dad barked, making me jump.

'What?' I mumbled, feeling my eyes sting.

He stopped abruptly and looked at me with a bit more sympathy, which was a good job because I'd had enough waterworks in one evening, thank you very much. 'So what's wrong with you? Mrs Platini says you've only been like this since Christmas, and don't go telling me it's because I left because I'm not having that. I was only back for a week!'

When I didn't reply, we began to walk on, but really slowly, like old people. 'I told you why I had to go. You seemed to understand,' Dad continued more softly.

Understand? I didn't think I did, really, not deep down, but I wasn't meant to admit that, was I? I was meant to say, 'Yeah, Dad, yeah, Mum, you two do whatever you want. Spend all our money on things we don't need? No problem! Leave us on Christmas Day because you can't hack it? Why not?' Oh, but by the way, Sammie, you'd better not mess up, only we're allowed to do that.

'Come on, Sammie, I'm being very patient here. I don't like the idea of you being rude to your teachers. You've been brought up better than that,' Dad goes.

For the first time ever, I began to feel angry with him. What did he expect? Dad was acting just like Mum had on Christmas Day, wanting me to tell him what he wanted to hear. That I didn't mind that he'd left; that my bad behaviour wasn't his fault.

I gave another sigh. Couldn't he just change the subject? I hardly saw him as it was and I didn't want to waste time arguing with him when I did. What if he died like Lloyd's grandad had and my last memory of him was this conversation? It could happen; those fork-lift trucks he uses at work could crush a man just like that. The thought made me shudder. 'I just don't like school; I'm allergic,' I said.

'Well, we all have to do things we don't like.

It's called life, and life's hard sometimes.'

'Life's a sandwich,' I muttered.

'What?'

'Life's a sandwich. That's what I compare it to.'

'How does that work?'

'You wouldn't get it.'

'Try me.'

'OK. Before Christmas, home was one slice of bread and school was another and After School club was the 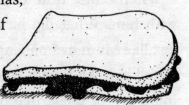 chocolate spread that made it taste nice. During Christmas, home was both slices and you were meant to be the chocolate spread because you were back, but that didn't work out, did it?'

It was Dad's turn to sigh this time. 'And now?'

'Now it's just bread and bread's all right but it's boring on its own and that's why I can't be bothered about school because there's nothing in between to make me want to eat it. Not that I want to eat school, if you know what I mean . . .'

Dad reached out and pinched my cheek which

meant he wasn't so cross at me and I reached up and pinched his cheek which meant I wasn't as cross at him. 'I hear you,' he goes. 'My life's like that too these days. A bit stale and curly round the edges.'

We walked the rest of the way in silence. It wasn't a bad silence, though.

When we reached the front door, I gave him the After School club brochures and newsletters. They'd only have made me sad if I'd kept them and Mum would have asked why I'd got them. She was very sensitive to anything that reminded her of owing money. 'Something to read on the bus,' I told him.

He took them and nodded towards the house. 'How's everything in there?'

'OK. A bit quieter now that Mum and Gemma don't argue no more. Mum's still sticking to her list—she's on number six.'

'That's good,' he said.

'She should be on number seven soon because she's increasing her hours at the pub.'

'Oh. Well, I'm impressed—you can tell her

that from me. And relieved—but don't tell her that!'

'I won't,' I said, then I promised I'd be more polite to Mrs Platini.

'I know you will,' he said, 'and I promise I'll think about the bread thing.'

Then he kissed me goodnight and left.

Chapter Thirty-Two

Another week passed. Another school day ended, only this time I hadn't been told off by Mrs Platini because I'd been good. A promise is a promise.

Automatically, I began tidying my tray. I know this sounds awful, but since I'd met up with everyone at the After School club again, and found out that they'd had a bad Christmas too, I felt better about my Christmas.

The downside was I wanted to see them all again.

I knew I couldn't, so half past three was agony and I had to do something to keep myself occupied. If I didn't, I'd torture myself with thoughts like: Mrs Fryston will be standing at the top of the steps greeting everyone . . . Brandon will be eating his green sweets . . . If only I could see Lloyd to talk to him. I wanted to do that more than anything.

I'd sent him a card. I'd found a picture of a child's magic set in the toy section of the Argos catalogue and cut that out and stuck it on the front. I thought Lloyd would appreciate the home-made effect. It wasn't the same as seeing him, though.

I let out a long sigh and carefully placed my pencil case neatly along the side of my dictionary. 'You've got that compulsive obsessive thing,' Aimee sneered.

Naz nodded in agreement. 'I know the thing you mean. There was a telly programme about it. Did you see it? There was that woman who washes her hands a thousand times a day and that footballer who has to lace his boots in a certain way before the beginning of a match.'

'Yeah,' Aimee agreed, nudging me, 'that's this one here.'

'It is not!' I said dully.

She flicked at my pencil case, sending it skew-whiff across my books just to test me out. Naz had a rummage for waxy bits in his ear-hole then continued, 'It wasn't as good as that programme about that other thing. Necra-something, where people just conk out every few minutes. Did you see that? This woman fell face first into her dinner. Gravy down her neck—the lot. It was hilarious.'

'Sounds it,' I said, dead sarky. There was a tap on my shoulder and I looked up to see Sam.

I frowned at him, puzzled. 'Come on,' he said, 'we're waiting.'

'What do you mean?'

'After School club.'

I glanced up. There was Mrs McCormack, smiling and nodding at me by the doorway.

'I don't go now,' I said, confused.

'Come on,' Sam repeated, 'I've got a new consignment of sweets to price up.'

I couldn't figure it out. Maybe Mrs Fryston had

changed her mind and wanted Pen returning, I thought to myself as I scraped back my chair. That'd be it. She wants Pen returning and needs to talk to me about it. That's a pity. I needed Pen for my plan for next Christmas but . . .

'Hi, Mrs McCormack,' I said as I walked over to her.

'Hello, Sammie. Welcome back,' she beamed, ticking me off her roster.

Weird.

It got even weirder inside the mobile. Guess who was standing having a natter to Mrs Fryston? Only my dad! 'What's going on?' I asked.

'Hello, Sammie,' Mrs Fryston beamed, 'have you met our new playworker?'

Chapter Thirty-Three

You could have knocked me down with a noodle!
My dad—working at After School club? No way!
But it was true. This is how it happened, right.
Remember I gave Dad the brochure to take home
with him? Inside the newsletter was only an appeal
for part-time help-out on a casual basis. Filling in
for holidays and illnesses and things like that. So
Dad thought, Why don't I go for it? I get to see
Sammie more, Sammie gets to see me and continues
at After School club at the same time. Bingo! So he
had phoned Mrs Fryston and enquired and she'd
said: 'Great, we need a bit of male influence. When

can you start?' Dad said, 'Whenever you like, depending on what shift I'm on.' Result!

It turned out it won't be for a few weeks, though, because he has to be checked out first to make sure he's not got a police record or nothing. The best bit was, it meant I could come back to After School club for free because Dad said he didn't want paying. 'Does Mum know about all this?' I asked.

Dad nodded. 'Yes, I talked it through with her on the phone. She's happy if you're happy.'

'Do—do I start tonight then?' I asked, my voice sounding all high and squeaky.

'Would you like to?' Mrs Fryston asked.

I looked round. Sam was unloading new tubs of sweets onto his tuck shop counter, shaking his head in disgust because the order would be wrong, bet you. Over by the book corner, Alex was playing on the giant 'four-in-a-row' with Tasmim and another Year Four, giggling away. Lloyd was at the computer he always sits at, the place next to him saved for Reggie. On top of the computer, I could see the card I'd sent. I can't tell you how good that made me feel.

Behind me, I heard the door slam open and Reggie calling to Brody, 'Told you I could beat you! You need more Weetabix, lass.'

This was followed by a yell as Brody thumped him. 'Cheat! I said on the count of three!' They were still arguing! That meant they were still going out with each other. Everything was as it should be.

I smiled to myself. I felt as if I'd been brought in from a storm and a soft blanket had been wrapped round me.

'OK,' I said to Mrs Fryston, 'I'll stay.'

She didn't look one bit surprised. 'Excellent. Right, I'll leave you to it, Sammie. I think you know where everything is!'

'Yep,' I said.

Dad wiggled his eyebrows as I looked up at him. 'Enough chocolate spread?' he asked.

'Just about,' I replied.

I felt something tug at my sweatshirt and looked down to see Brandon smiling up at me. 'Hey up, Thammie!' he lisped.

'You've lost a tooth!' I said, noticing the black gap immediately.

'Yeth. I did it at dinnertime. Do you want to thee it? It'th thtill got blood on it.'

'Cool,' I said.

'Come on then,' he goes, dragging me away, 'it'th in my lunchbokth. In fact, it'th in my apple.'

'I'll . . . er . . . see you later, Sammie,' Dad said.

'OK.'

What do you mean, is that it? He's my dad. We don't need words.

Epilogue

I was going to say that after a few days it was as if nothing had changed. I was back in my old routine like before Christmas. You know, home, school, After School club, but that wouldn't be true. It's miles better!

It's not just because Dad's at After School club. I hardly see him, if I'm honest. Brandon kind of baggied him in the first week and hasn't let go of him since. I don't mind a bit; just knowing Dad is in the mobile is good enough for me. Besides, I'm too busy doing my homework in Boff Corner to have time to chat. Don't faint! Mrs Platini can't

ZETLAND AVENUE
PRIMARY SCHOOL.

CERTIFICATE
OF
REWARD

This is to certify that
Sammie Wesley

has been awarded a gold star
for work and a certificate

believe it, either. I don't know how many reward certificates I've had since parents' evening but I'm running out of space on my bedroom wall to put them.

Boff Corner was Sam's idea, though Reggie gave it the title. What happened was, Mrs Fryston said she wanted to change the mobile round and create 'zones' to zap the place up a bit. Sam suggested a homework zone so anyone who wanted to could get their school work done in peace instead of having to wait until they got home and were too tired.

Mrs Fryston thought it was a great idea and set it all up. At first, only Sam used it, but one day I had some maths that I just couldn't do, so I asked Sam for help and he explained it miles better than Mrs Platini had. After that, I was in Boff Corner every evening. I try not to bug Sam too much when I'm stuck but he doesn't seem to mind. I told him if his greeting card business goes down the pan for ever because of the flood and he has nothing to inherit, he could always go into teaching when he was older because he's a natural.

A couple of days after I started using Boff Corner, Lloyd joined us. He'd been very quiet since his grandad had died and at first he just sat and read or drew birds and animals in his sketch pad without saying much. He's a brilliant drawer, by the way. You should see his birds—they look as if they could fly off the page.

Anyway, it's really cosy in Boff Corner because it's surrounded on three sides by bookcases so you feel closed in and private. I think that's why Lloyd opened up to us one day. He told us about how he felt about his grandad and what the funeral had been like and how he believes his grandad is watching over him.

'Like a guardian angel?' Sam asked.

'Or a fairy?' I asked.

Lloyd said no to both those suggestions but we had a really good discussion about death right until home time.

I suppose now I've mentioned fairies again you

want to know what I've done with Pen. Well, you don't have to worry: she's safe and sound and living in my knicker drawer. Mrs Fryston knows I've still got her and she said that's fine as long as I remember to bring her back next Christmas. I try not to disturb Pen because I know she has to rest until next Christmas when she becomes magic again.

I can't wait for next Christmas. I'll get my wish right this time. I'll make it clear and specific. That's where it went wrong last time, you see. I didn't think it through clearly enough. 'Bring Dad home,' I said but I didn't add, 'and make him stay and make him and Mum fall in love with each other again.'

I'm not saying that's what I'll wish for next time. I can see now that Mum and Dad are happier apart. There's no point wasting my wishes, is there? Mum and Gemma have started arguing again, so maybe I'll use my wish on them. Gemma really has started hanging out at the bus terminus now *and* she smokes! Still, that's what she should be doing, isn't it, if she's going to be a proper

Teenager from Hell? Not the smoking—that's disgusting and makes her stink—I mean rebelling.

No, I think I'll keep my wish simple next time or I might be generous and pass it on to someone else instead. Someone like Brody. She told me the other day her year has been getting worse and worse since Christmas instead of better and better like mine. In fact, I think I'll go check out how she is now, if you don't mind . . .

See you,

luv, Sammie

The girls are back...

Life sucks!

*Everyone's always depending on me—Brody the Reliable.
Expecting me to sort out their problems, but when I need
help even my best buddy lets me down. Well, fine, if that's
how he wants to play it, he can take a hike.*

*And that goes for all the others too. I'm through doing
things just to please other people, and that includes
being captain for the Big Book Quiz. Let Mrs Fryston find
some other loser . . .*

ISBN-13: 978-0-19-275378-6
ISBN-10: 0-19-275378-9

What a nightmare!

All I want is a quiet life—but do you think that's possible?
No chance.

It started off fine. With one best friend and out-of-school stuff
kept to almost zero, I had no worries. But then it all went
wrong. First there was the secret, then the secret about the
secret . . . and now everything's out of control!

The only time I feel calm is when I'm talking to my brother
Daniel—at least he never answers back. OK, so he's been
dead for years, but I don't have a problem with that—
unfortunately my family obviously does . . .

ISBN-13: 978-0-19-275279-6
ISBN-10: 0-19-275279-7

It's crunch-time!

I'd been really looking forward to visiting Brody, Alex, and the rest of the gang—but now I'm not so sure I should have come at such a major time. My mum and stepdad, Darryl, aren't getting on. She's such an old nag—I don't know how Darryl puts up with her.

Well, if push comes to shove I know exactly where I want to be. And it's not with Mum, that's for sure. If she can divorce Darryl, then I'll divorce her—end of story! And until they sort it out I'm staying down here with my mates, even if it means doing another runner . . .

ISBN-13: 978-0-19-275380-9
ISBN-10: 0-19-275380-0

Helena Pielichaty (pronounced Pierre-li-hatty) was born in Stockholm, Sweden, but most of her childhood was spent in Yorkshire. Her English teacher wrote of her in Year Nine that she produced 'lively and quite sound work but she must be careful not to let the liveliness go too far.' Following this advice, Helena never took her liveliness further south than East Grinstead, where she began her career as a teacher. She didn't begin writing until she was 32. Since then, Helena has written many books for Oxford University Press. She lives in Nottinghamshire with her husband and two children.

www.helena-pielichaty.com